The Real Diary of a Real Boy

By

HENRY A. SHUTE

Applewood Books
Bedford, Massachusetts

The Real Diary of a Real Boy was first published in 1902 by The Everett Press of Boston, Massachusetts. The text of this printing is reproduced from a 1902 edition.

Front cover: Detail from "Crossing the Pasture" (1872) by Winslow Homer.

Thank you for purchasing an Applewood Book. Applewood reprints America's lively classics—books from the past that are still of interest to modern readers. For a free copy of our current catalog, write to: Applewood Books, P.O. Box 365, Bedford, MA 01730

ISBN 1-55709-531-0

Library of Congress Card Number: 00-110668

INTRODUCTION

In the winter of 1901–02, while rummaging an old closet in the shed-chamber of my father's house, I unearthed a salt-box which had been equipped with leather hinges at the expense of considerable ingenuity, and at a very remote period. In addition to this, a hasp of the same material, firmly fastened by carpet-tacks and a catch of bent wire, bade defiance to burglars, midnight marauders, and safe-breakers.

With the aid of a tack-hammer the combination was readily solved, and an eager examination of the contents of the box disclosed : —

1. Fish-line of braided shoemaker's thread, with perch hook, to which adhered the mummied remains of a worm that lived and flourished many, many years ago.

2. Popgun of pith elder and hoopskirt wire.

3. Horse-chestnut bolas, calculated to revolve in opposite directions with great velocity, by an up-and-down motion of the holder's

wrist ; also extensively used for the adornment of telegraph-wires, — there were no telephones in those days, — and the cause of great profanity amongst linemen.

4. More fish-hooks of the ring variety, now obsolete.

5. One blood alley, two chinees, a particolored glass agate, three pewees, and unnumbered drab-colored marbles.

6. Small bow of whalebone, with two arrows.

7. Six-inch bean-blower, for school use — a weapon of considerable range and great precision when used with judgment behind a Guyot's Common School Geography.

8. Unexpended ammunition for same, consisting of putty pellets.

9. Frog's hind leg, extra dry.

10. Wing of bluejay, very ditto.

11. Letter from "Beany," post-marked "Biddeford, Me.," and expressing great indignation because "Pewt" "hasent wrote."

12. Copy-book inscribed "Diry."

Introduction

The examination of this copy-book lasted the rest of the day, and it was read with the peculiar pleasure one experiences in reviewing some of the events of a happy boyhood.

With the earnest hope that others may experience a little of the pleasure I gained from the reading, I submit the "Diry" to the public.

HENRY A. SHUTE.

EXETER, N. H., *Sept. 23, 1902.*

THE
REAL DIARY
OF A
REAL BOY

FATHER thot i aught to keep a diry, but i sed i dident want to, because i coodent wright well enuf, but he sed he wood give $1000 dolars if he had kept a diry when he was a boy.

Mother said she gessed nobody wood dass to read it, but father said everybody would tumble over each other to read it, anyhow he would give $1000 dolars if he had kept it. I told him i would keep one regular if he would give me a quarter of a dolar a week, but he said i had got to keep it anyhow and i woodent get no quarter for it neither, but he woodent ask to read it for a year, and i know he will forget it before that, so 1 am going to wright just what i want to in it. Father always forgets everything but my lickins. he remembers them every time you bet.

So i have got to keep it, but it seems to me that my diry is worth a quarter of a dolar a week if fathers is worth $1000 dolars, everybody says father was a buster when he was a boy and went round with Gim Melcher and Charles Talor. my grandmother says i am the best boy she ever see, if i didn't go with Beany Watson and Pewter Purinton, it was Beany and Pewt made me tuf.

there dos'nt seem to be much to put into a diry only fites and who got licked at school and if it ranes or snows, so i will begin to-day.

December 1, 186– brite and fair, late to brekfast, but mother dident say nothing. father goes to boston and works in the custum house so i can get up as late as i want to. father says he works like time, but i went to boston once and father dident do anything but tell stories about what he and Gim Melcher usted to do when he was a boy. once or twice when a man came in they would all be wrighting fast, when the man came in again i sed why do you all wright so fast when he comes in and stop when he goes out, and the man sort of laffed and went out laffing, and the men were mad and told father not to bring that dam little fool again.

December 2. Skinny Bruce got licked in school today. I told my granmother about it and she said she was glad i dident do eny-

3

thing to get punnished for and she felt sure
i never wood. i dident tell her i had to stay
in the wood box all the morning with the
cover down. i dident tell father either you
bet.

December 2. rany. i forgot to say it raned
yesterday too. i got cold and have a red rag
round my gozzle.

December 2. pretty near had a fite in
schol today. Skinny Bruce and Frank Elliot
got rite up with there fists up when the bell
rung. it was two bad, it wood have been a
buly fite. i bet on Skinny.

December 3, 186— brite and fair. went to
church today. Me and Pewt and Beany go
to the Unitarial church. we all joined sunday school to get into the Crismas festerval.
they have it in the town hall and have two
trees and supper and presents for the scholars.

4

so we are going to stay til after crismas anyway the unitarials have jest built a new
church. Pewt and Beany's fathers painted it
and so they go there. i don't know why we
go there xcept because they don't have any
church in the afternoon. Nipper Brown and
Micky Gould go there. we all went into the
same class. our teacher is Mister Winsor a
student. we call them stewdcats. after we
had said our lesson we all skinned out with
Mr. Winsor. when we went down Maple
street we saw 2 roosters fiting in Dany Win-
gates yard, and we stoped to see it. i knew
more about fiting roosters than any of the
fellers, because me and Ed Towle had fit
roosters lots. Mr. Winsor said i was a sport,
well while the roosters were fiting, sunday
school let out and he skipped acros the street
and walked off with one of the girls and we

hollered for him to come and see the fite out, and he turned red and looked mad. the leghorn squorked and stuck his head into a corner. when a rooster squorks he wont fite any more.

December 5. snowed today and school let out at noon. this afternoon went down to the library to plug stewdcats. there was me and Beany and Pewt, and Whacker and Pozzy Chadwick and Pricilla Hobbs. Pricilla is a feller you know, and Pheby Talor, Pheby is a feller too, and Lubbin Smith and Nigger Bell, he is' nt a nigger only we call him Nigger, and Tommy Tompson and Dutchey Seamans and Chick Chickering, and Tady Finton and Chitter Robinson.

December 6. Gim Wingate has got a new bobtail coat.

December 7, 186– Got sent to bed last

nite for smoking hayseed cigars and can't go
with Beany enny more. It is funny, my father
wont let me go with Beany becaus he is tuf,
and Pewts father wont let Pewt go with me
becaus im tuf, and Beanys father says if he
catches me or Pewt in his yard he will lick
time out of us. Rany today.

December 8. Skinny Bruce got licked in
school today. Skipy Moses was in the wood
box all the morning.

December 9. brite and fair, speakin day
today. missed in Horatius at the brige.

December 10. Clowdy but no rane. went
to church. lots of new fellers in sunday
school. me and Beany and Pewt and Pile
Woods and Billy Folsom and Jimmy Gad
and lots of others. Mister Winsor dident
teach today, gess they woodent let him on
account of the rooster fite.

7

The Real Diary

December 11. My new boots from Tommy Gads came today. i tell you they are clumpers. no snow yet.

December 12. Crismas is pretty near, dont know wether i shall get ennything. father says i dont desirve ennything. you can get goozeberrys down to Si Smiths 1 dozen for 5 cents. He has a funny sine it is

flour
meal
molasses
sugar
coffee
tea
spises
pork &
lard
salt

8

butter

ham

eggs

&so

December 15. Fite at recess today, Gran Miller and Ben Rundlet. Ben licked him easy. the fellers got to stumping each other to fite. Micky Gould said he cood lick me and i said he want man enuf and he said if i wood come out behind the school house after school he wood show me and i said i wood and all the fellers hollered and said they wood be there. But after school i thaught i aught to go home and split my kindlings and so i went home. a feller aught to do something for his family ennyway. i cood have licked him if i had wanted to.

December 16. Tady Finton got licked in school today. snowed today a little.

December 17. rained in the nite and then snowed a little. it was auful slipery and coming out of church Squire Lane fell down whak and Mr. Burley cought hold of the fence and his feet went so fast that they seemed all fuzzy, i tell you if he cood run as fast as that he cood run a mile a minite.

December 18. brite and fair. nothing particilar. o yes, Skinny Bruce got licked in school.

December 19. Cold as time. Went to a sosiable tonite at the Unitarial vestry. cant go again because Keene told mother i was impident to the people. i want impident. you see they was making poetry and all sitting around the vestry. they wanted to play copenhagin and post office and clap in and clap

10

out, but Mister Erl woodent let them because
it was in church. so they had to play poetry.
one person wood give a word and then the
oppisite person would give a word that rimed
with it. it was auful silly. a girl would give
the word direxion and then a stewdcat would
say affexion and waul his eyes towards the
girl. and then another wood say miss, and
another stewdcat wood say kiss and then he
wood waul his eyes, and when it came my
turn i said what rimes with jellycake, and
the girls turned red and the stewdcats looked
funny, and Mister Burley said if i coodent
behave i had better go home. Keene needent
have told mother anyway. You jest wait
Keene, and see what will happen some day.

December 20. Bully skating. went after
school and skated way up to the eddy, was
going to skate with Lucy Watson but Pewt

and Beany hollered so that i dident dass to. Johnny Toomey got hit with a hocky block rite in the snoot and broke his nose.

December 21. Brite and fair. nothing particular to-day. nobody got licked. old Francis had his hand done up in a sling. he said he had a bile on it. i tell you the fellers were glad.

December 22. Warm and rany and spoiled the skating. coodent do anything but think of Crismas.

December 23. Saturday and no skating. went down to the library to get a book for sunday. me and Beany were sticking pins into the fellers and making them holler and Jo Parsons the libarian jumped rite over the counter and chased us way down to Mr. Hams coffin shop. he dident catch us either. then we went down town and Billy Swett

12

lent me a dime novel to read sunday. it was named Billy Bolegs a sequil to Nat Tod the traper. sequil means the things in Nat Tod that was not finished.

December 24. Brite and fair. Crismas tomorrow. went to sunday school. Mr. Lovel is our teacher now.

December 25. Crismas. got a new nife, a red and white scarf and a bag of Si Smiths goozeberies. pretty good for me.

December 26. Crismas tree at the town hall. had supper and got a bag of candy and a long string of pop corn. Mr. Lovel took off the presents and his whiskers caught fire, and he hollered o hell right out. that was pretty good for a sunday school teacher, wasent it. Jimmy Gad et too much and was sick.

December 27. Beany has got a new striped

shirt not a false bosom but a whole shirt.
Beany wont speak to me now. Lucy Watson
has got a new blew hat with a fether. she
wont speak to Keene and Cele eether. you
jest wait Beany and Lucy and see.

Jan. 1, 186– Had an awful time in school
today. me and Cawcaw Harding set together.
when we came in from resess Cawcaw reached
over and hit me a bat, and i lent him one in
the snoot, and he hit me back. we was jest
fooling, but old Francis called Cawcaw up
front to lick him. i thought if i went up and
told him he wood say, noble boy go to your
seat, i wont lick neether of you. anyway i
knew that Cawcaw wood tell on me, and so i
told old Francis i hit Cawcaw first, and old
Francis said Harry i have had my eye on you
for a long time, and he jest took us up and
slammed us together, and then he wood put

14

me down and shake Cawcaw and then he
wood put Cawcaw down and shake me till
my head wabbled and he turned me upside
down and all the fellers looked upside down
and went round and round and somehow i
felt silly like and kind of like laffin. i dident
want to laff but coodent help it. and then
he talked to us and sent us to our seats and
told us to study, and i tried to but all the
words in the book went round and round
and i felt awful funny and kind of wabbly,
and when i went home mother said something was the matter and i told her and
then i cried, i don't know what i cried for,
becaus i dident ake any. father said he
wood lick me at home when i got licked at
school and perhaps that was why i cried.
ennyway when father come home i asked
him if he was a going to lick me and he

15

said not by a dam sight, and he gave me ten
cents and when i went to bed i got laffin and
crying all to once, and coodent stop, and
mother set in my room and kept her hand on
my forred until i went to sleep. i drempt i
was fiting all the time. when i get big enuf
there is going to be a fite between me and
old Francis, you see if there aint.

Jan. 2, Me and Beany has made up. i
told him i had ten cents and then he dident
feel so big about his new shirt. ennyway we
went down to Si Smiths and got a dozen
goozeberries and then went down to doctor
Derborns and got a glass of sody water and
took turns drinking it and seeing which cood
gulp the loudest. Beany beat.

Jan. 3. brite and fair. Went down to
Pewts tonite to make hayseed cigars. We
made 5 kinds, hayseed, sweet firn, cornsilk,

mullin leeves, and grape vine. my mouth taisted aufuly all nite.

Jan. 4 brite and fair. Pewt dident come to school today. i gess he was sick. my mouth taisted aufuly all day.

Jan. 5. clowdy and aufuly cold. Pewt came to school today and got a licking for puting gum on Nigger Bells seat. Nig set in it til it dride and then tride to get up and coodent. then old Francis come down the ile and snaiked Nigger out and when he see the gum he asked us who put it there. we all said we dident, but he licked Pewt becaus he had seen Pewt chooing gum.

Jan. 6. it snowed last nite and today. Speaking in school today. i spoke the berrial of sir John More. old Francis said he never heard ennything wirse in his life. i

17

hope he wont tell father. this afternoon we pluged stewdcats.

Jan. 7 Ed Towle has got a gote. the fellers stumped me to hold him by the horns and he buted me over in the slosh. mother said i had no bisiness to be playing on sunday.

Jan. 8. brite and fair. there is going to be a nigger show in the town hall tonite. father says i cant go becaus i sassed aunt Sarah. it is uncle Toms cabbin.

Jan. 9. brite and fair. Beany went to the nigger show. he led one of the bludhouns in the prosession and got a ticket. Beany had on a red coat jest like the dogs. he said it was buly.

Jan. 10 rany. Nipper Brown is the best scolar in my class. i am the wirst. i can lick Nipper easy.

18

Jan. 11. brite and fair. After school me and Beany and Pewt and Fatty Melcher and Pozzy Chadwick and lots of fellers went skating on fresh river. i was skating backwerd and i got one leg in a eal hole, gosh the water was cold and before i got home my britches leg was all froze.

Jan. 12. nobody got licked in school today, gess why, becaus there wassent enny school. old Francis was sick, i went skating.

Jan. 13. brite and — no it was rany. had a speling mach today in school. Cele and Genny Morrison staid up til the last and then Cele missed and set down balling, and Genny beat. i cant stop to wright enny more becaus i am going to the levee with father.

Jan. 14, 186– Went to a big levee last nite

at the town hall. Bill Morrill and Nuel Head
and Dave Quimby and Frank Hervey got it
up. they had Hook and Pasons quadril band
of Haverhil. father bought a ticket becaus he
was in the custum house and has to be frends
with people. it was splendid. most everybody went all dressed up in blue silk and
red and crokay slippers. Ham Perkins and
Charlie Lane and Charley Piper and Chick
Randall and Dan Ranlet and Grace Morril
and the Head girls and Sweat girls and
Carrie Towle and Sarah Foster, J. Arthur
Fosters sister and the Melcher boys and they
all hopped round pretty lively, i tell you.
i staid until 12 o'clock and listened to the
band. i never had so good time in my life.

Jan. 15. i am all spekled over. mother
says she is afrade i have got chicken pocks.
i gess i have been in the hen koop to mutch.

Jan. 16. the speckels have all gone of. doctor Perry says i et to many donuts.

Jan. 18. brite and fair. yesterday to and day before yesterday i have forgot.

Jan. 19. snowed all day. Me and Beany is mad.

Jan. 20. father is sick becaus he et to mutch salt fish and potato and pork. he is auful cross and hit me a bat today becaus i left the door open. i gess he will be sorry when i am ded.

Jan. 21. brite and fair. went to church in the morning and in the afternoon greeced some paper and trased some pictures.

Jan. 22. i had to stay in the woodbox today for whispering to Whacker with the cover down. i like it becaus they is a peep hole in the box and you can see the fellers and they cant see you. by and by Gimmy

Fitsgerald whispered and old Francis put him in to and we took turns peeping.

Jan. 23. it raned hard all day and we had one sesion. Beany came over and we made up and plaid in the barn making fly boxes.

Jan. 24. nothing much today, rany in the morning and froze at night.

Jan. 25. brite and fair. everything was covered with ice and when father started for the depot he tumbled down the front steps from the top to the botom. mother says he went bumpity bump and his hat went one way and his dinner box went the other. i herd him swaring aufuly about that dam boy, and i gess he wood have come up and licked time out of me, but he had to hurry to get the train.

22

Jan. 26. jest as soon as the skating comes it has to snow and spoil it.

Jan. 27. i coodent go out of the yard this afternoon becaus i dident put ashes on the front steps before father fell down and so Pewt and Beany and Whacker and Nibby Hartwell and Diddly Colket and Nipper and Prisilla and Gim Wingit and lots of the fellers came over and we had a snowball fite. mother says she hops father wont keep me at home anuther afternoon.

Jan. 28. brite and fair. it never ranes sundays so a feller cant go to church

Jan. 29. Nothing puticular today. it always seams harder to go to school mundays, more fellers gets licked mundays than enny day in the weak. i got stood on the platform with my head in the corner for looking of my book today.

23

Jan. 30. brite and fair. i have got a auful chilblane on my heel.

Jan. 31. brite and fair. i was glad today was wensday in the afternoon i went skating. the students played baseball on the ice.

Feb. 1. brite and fair. pretty soon it will be Washintons berthday, and then all the boys can ring the town bell at noon and at nite.

Feb. 2. clowdy but no snow. tomorror will be saterday they is only 2 days in the weak that is wirth ennything and that is wensday and saterday except in vacation.

Feb. 3. Snowed like time all the forenoon. in the afternoon me and Pewt and Beany rolled up some big snowballs. then tonite we put all the balls together and made a big snowman rite in front of Mrs. Lewises front door. then we put a old hat on it and

24

hung a peace of paper on it and wrote man
wanted on the paper. tomorrow all the people who go to church will see it and laff
because Mister Lewis got a devorse. they
will be some fun tomorrow.

Feb. 5. i coodent wright ennything last
nite becaus i got sent to bed and got a licking. i tell you we got in a auful scrape.
sunday morning me and Pewt and Beany
went out erly to see our snowman. he was
there and when people began to go by they
began to laff, and most of the people said it
was the funniest thing they ever see and
who ever put it there was a pretty smart
feller. so we said we did it and Pewt said
he thought of it ferst and Beany said he did,
and i said i did most of the werk.

Well, pretty soon some people came along
and looked at it and said it was a shame and

they went over to pull of the paper and she came out and see it, and she took a broom and nocked it over and broke it all up. and then she went rite down to my house to tell father. then she went over to Beanys house and then up to Pewts. well after church father took me over to her house, and Beany was there with his father and Pewt with his father. she said she wood have us arested for it. but they talked a long time and after a while she said if our fathers wood lick us and make us saw and split a cord of wood she woodent say no more about it. when we went out father said, i never see such dam boys did you Brad, did you Wats, and they said they never did. so we have got to saw and split that wood and we got licked two.

Feb. 6. brite and fair. me and Pewt and

26

Beany sawed and split some wood for Misses Lewis.

Feb. 7. brite and fair. sawed some more wood, me and Pewt and Beany.

Feb. 8. brite and fair. split some more wood, me and Pewt and Beany.

Feb. 9. Fatty Melcher and Cawcaw Harding, Chitter Robinson and Medo Thurston helped saw some more wood.

Feb. 10. Brite and fair. this afternoon Whack Pozzy and Boog Chadwick, Dutchy Semans, Nigger Bell Pop Clark, Shinny Thing and Pile Wood all come down with saws and axes and helped us saw that wood, we worked all the afternoon and got it done and piled up before dark. then Misses Lewis asked us in and gave us some buly donuts and some sweatened water and we sung and told stories and before we went we told her

27

we was sorry we bilt the snowman and she said she was sorry two. then when we went away we give 3 cheers for her.

Feb. 11. brite and fair. i shant forget last sunday very soon.

Feb. 12. rany today. i dont care becaus i havent got to saw enny more wood.

Feb. 13. still rany. i dont care.

Feb. 14. pretty cold today. going to have a new kind of speling mach tomorrow.

Feb. 15. Got to the head in spelling to-day. old Francis makes us all stand up in the ile and gives us a lot of words to spell and then we wright them down on our slates and then the head feller or girl changes slates with the foot feller or girl and so on and then old Francis wrights the words on the blackboard and then we mark each others slates. John Flanygin was the foot feller and had my slate. well most of Johns words was wrong. but John marked mine all write. i gess John dident know it, but ther was 4 or 5 of my words speled wrong. i set out to tell old Francis but dident dass to becaus he licked me for teling that i paisted Caw-caw Harding that time. so i kept still and kept at the head and John kept at the foot. i hope John will do it again tomorrow.

Feb. 16. Beat in speling today.

Feb. 17. beat in speling today.

Feb. 19. beat in speling today. old Francis is a going to give a prise tomorrow. i told father i was pretty sure to get it and he said it will be the first one. Aunt Sarah asked him if he took many prises. and he said he dident get much of a prise when he got me. i gess he wont say that tomorrow when i bring my prise home.

29

Feb. 20. i dident get the prise. you see yesterday John Flanygin spelt more words write than Gimmy Fitsgerald and Gimmy went to the foot. when we marked slates Gimmy marked 9 of my words wrong out of 20, and I had to go down most to where John Flannygin was. old Francis said he dident beleave i had aught to have staid at the head so long as i did and i was afraid he would lick me and John but he dident. he said he was ashamed and disapointed in me but i gess he was not the only one who was disapointed. i had told Pewt and Beany i wood treat on what father wood give me for getting the prise. Pewt and Beany was both mad, and are going to lay for Gimmy.

Feb. 21, i forgot to say what the wether was most every day this weak. it has been brite and fair most of the time, only it snowed two days and raned most of one day. brite and fair to-day and cold as time.

Feb. 23, Clowdy and cold. Pop Clark had to crawl through a chair to-day. he went through so fast old Francis only hit him 2 bats. Tady Finton and Nigger Bell both got licked. Tady dident cry or holler a bit, but Nigger hollered just like a girl. i supposed Nigger was more of a man than that.

Feb. 24, Beany and Pewt got punching today in school and old Francis made them stand on the platform with their arms round each others neck all the forenoon. i bet they felt pretty cheep. Brite and fair.

Feb. 25, i have got a new pair of britches at erl and Cutts. i gess Beany aint the only one which has good clothes eather.

Feb. 26. Nothing particular today. Went down to old Heads shop to see the stewd-

cats ride velosipedes. There is going to be a
race in the town hall tomorrow night.

Feb. 27. Father said i cood go to the
velosipede race if i woodent miss splitting
my kindlings for a week. i did miss them
twice but mother did0 tell him and if he
dont ask her before tonight i am all right.

Feb. 28. Last night went to the velosipede race. it was jest ripping. i got down
before the door opened. Bob Carter came
pretty soon but he woodent let us in until
the ticket man came. Mr. Watson was the
ticket man and he let me and Beany and
Shinny Thing in free. they had a lot of seats
in the center of the hall, and the rest round
the edges, and a open track around the hall.
On the platform set Bill Morrill and Dave
Quimby and John Getchell and Eben Folsom. Most of the fellers in the race were

stewdcats and most of the stewdcats and the girls had the seats in the center of the hall. The stewdcats who were to race were Stone and Stuart and Lee and Clifford and August Belmont and Swift and Nichols and George Kent and Cutler and Johnny Heald and Gear and Burly and Bob Morison. the townies were Charlie Gerish and Doctor Prey. each feller rode round the hall twice to get going like time, and then Dave Quimby hollered go and he had to ride around the hall until he had rid a quarter of a mile.

When the stewdcats rode all the other stewdcats yelled and the girls waved their handkerchiefs and the band played and the excitement was dreadful.

After a while Docter Prey came out and all the townies got up and cheered and the band played the star spangled banner, because

Doctor fit in the war, and Doctor took of his hat and bowed and then rode round like time. he rode faster than most every one of them except Stone and Stuart and Lee and Clifford and Belmont and Swift. i gess if Doc hadent fit so hard in the war he wood have beat them all. and then Charlie Gerish came out and all the townies hollered again and Charlie made his legs go so fast that they coodent hardly see them, and jest before the last time around his velosipede slipped and Charlie went fluking over three settees. he jumped on his velosipede again and went around with his britches all torn but he dident get around quite quick enuf to beat Stone, then the townies yelled and said it was a cheat and the stewdcats hissed, and some of the townies said they could lick the stewdcats, and the stewdcats said they

34

wasent man enuf and it looked as if there was a going to be a row when Charlie Gerrish got up and said he was beat fair and there wasent enything to get mad about, and that he would like to shake hands with the stewdcat which beat him, and he wood like to race him another time but he coodent then because he hurt his leg, and then they shook hands and every one felt buly, and the stewdcats said hooray for Charlie and the townies hollered hooray for Stone, and Bill Morrill made a speech and give the prise to Stone and the band played and we all went home. i bet Doc. Prey and Charlie Gerrish can lick any two stewdcats in the hall.

Mar. 2. i went to a show in the town hall tonight. it was a singing show called the haymakers. it was splendid. Mr. Gale got it up. they have been practising all winter.

Alice Gewell was a dary maid and Charlie Lane was a katydid, and lots of others sung. it was splendid.

Mar. 3. Cloudy but no rane. went down to Langley's store for some juju paste, saw a fite. Old Kize tried to arest Bill Hartnit and Bill lammed time out of him and after a while old Swain came up and arrested him.

Mar. 4. Brite and fair. Went to church to-day, the fernace smoked so the people had to come home. They say they will have it fixed before next sunday. i hope not.

Mar. 5. School closes tomorrow. i got kept after school tonight for whispering to Cawcaw.

Mar. 6. School closed today and we voted for prises. Mister Gordon give 4 prizes for the 2 best fellers and 2 best girls for the term. So we voted for them. Most of the

fellers wanted to vote for Jenny Morrison
because she was the prettiest girl there
and can go the greeshun bend better than
enny girl in the school. and most of the
girls dident like Jenny Morrison and wanted
to vote for Dora Moses and Mary Luverin,
and the girls wanted to vote for Lees Moses
because he was polite to them and rather go
with the girls than the boys and we holler
at him, but he can fite for i saw him lick
Gim Erly one day, and Gim Erly can rassle
better than enny one but Jack Melvil. well
most of the fellows wanted to vote for Tady
Finton or Pop Clark or Skinny Bruce because they never get mad or cry when they
are licked and make lots of fun, but we
knew they coodent get the prize for they
are all the time raising time and getting
licked and so we voted for Honey Donovan

37

and Moses Gordon, and when the votes was counted Dora Moses and Mary Luvering got the prizes for the girls and Mose Gordon and Nigger Bell for the boys. That was all write about Dora Moses and Mary Luverin because they was the best girls and always went together, but we dident like it very well about Mose and Nigger, only we thought that so long as Mose's father give the prizes Mose ought to have one. i gess most of the girls must have voted for Nig, because they was mad with Lees Moses. i know what they was mad at too.

Then the first class give old Francis a present of some books and when he turned over the leaves there was twenty dollars there, and old Francis was surprised and made a fine speech, and the people all clapped becaus he made such a good speech.

38

i heard him saying it over the night before
when i was kept after school. No school
for 2 weeks.

Mar. 7. When my father was a boy he
was the best fiter in this town.

Mar. 9. Went down to Fatty Melchers today to make a violin, we cut a piece of wood
the shape of a violin then take some horse-
hairs and strech them over a brige and you
can play a tune on them. in school i learnt
to play on a piece of india rubber. you pull
a piece of elastic out of your congres boot
and hold it in your teeth and pull it tite and
snap it with your fingers and you can play
tunes that you can hear but no one else can.
old Francis saw me snapping the elastic and
came and took it away. i have got plenty
more in my boot. i am saving money to buy
me a cornet. when i get enuf i am a going
to play in the band.   **39**

The Real Diary

Mar. 10. plesent day. old Si Smiths big white dog and a bull dog had an awful fite today. neether licked and they had to squert water on them to seperate them. they dident make no noise, only jest hung write on to each others gozzles. my aunt Sarah said it was dredful, and she staid to the window to see how dredful it was.

Mar. 11, 186– Went to church in the morning. the fernace was all write. Mister Lennard preeched about loving our ennymies, and told every one if he had any angry feelings towards ennyone to go to him and shake hands and see how much better you wood feel. i know how it is becaus when me and Beany are mad we dont have eny fun and when we make up the one who is to blam always wants to treet. why when Beany was mad with me becaus i went home from

40

Gil Steels surprise party with Lizzie Towle,
Ed Towles sister, he woodent speak to me
for 2 days, and when we made up he
treated me to ice cream with 2 spoons and
he let me dip twice to his once. he took
pretty big dips to make up. Beany is mad if
enny of the fellers go with Lizzie Towle.
she likes Beany better than she does enny of
the fellers and Beany ought to be satisfied,
but sometimes he acks mad when i go down
there to fite roosters with Ed. i gess he
needent worry much, no feller isnt going to
leave of fiting roosters to go with no girls.
well i most forgot what i was going to say,
but after church i went up to Micky Gould
who was going to fite me behind the school
house, and said Micky lets be friends and
Micky said, huh old Skinny, i can lick you
in 2 minits and i said you aint man enuf

and he called me a nockneed puke, and i
called him a wall eyed lummix and he give me
a paist in the eye and i gave him a good one
in the mouth, and then we rassled and Micky
threw me and i turned him, and he got hold
of my new false bosom and i got hold of his
hair, and the fellers all hollered hit him
Micky, paist him Skinny, and Mister Puring-
ton, Pewts father pulled us apart and i had
Mickys paper collar and necktie and some of
his hair and he had my false bosom and
when i got home father made me go to bed
and stay there all the afternoon for fiting,
but i gess he dident like my losing my false
bosom. ennyway he asked me how many
times i hit Micky and which licked. he let
me get up at supper time. next time i try
to love my ennymy i am a going to lick
him first.

42

Went to a sunday school concert in the evening. Keene and Cele sung now i lay me down to sleep. they was a lot of people sung together and Mister Gale beat time. Charlie Gerish played the violin and Miss Packerd sung. i was scart when Keene and Cele sung for i was afraid they would break down, but they dident, and people said they sung like night horks. i gess if they knowed how night horks sung they woodent say much. father felt pretty big and to hear him talk you wood think he did the singing. he give them ten cents apeace. i dident get none. you gest wait, old man till i get my cornet.

Went to a corcus last night. me and Beany were in the hall in the afternoon helping Bob Carter sprinkle the floor and put on the sordust. the floor was all shiny

with wax and aufully slipery. so Bob got
us to put on some water to take off the
shiny wax. well write in front of the platform there is a low platform where they get
up to put in their votes and then step down
and Beany said, dont put any water there
only jest dry sordust. so i dident. well that
night we went erly to see the fun. Gim
Luverin got up and said there was one man
which was the oldest voter in town and he
ought to vote the first, the name of this des-
tinkuished sitizen was John Quincy Ann
Pollard. then old mister Pollard got up and
put in his vote and when he stepped down
his heels flew up and he went down whak on
the back of his head and 2 men lifted him up
and lugged him to a seat, and then Ed Der-
born, him that rings the town bell, stepped
up pretty lively and went flat and swore

44

terrible, and me and Beany nearly died we laffed so. well it kept on, people dident know what made them fall, and Gim Odlin sat write down in his new umbrella and then they sent me down stairs for a pail of wet sordust and when i was coming up i heard an awful whang, and when i got up in the hall they were lugging old mister Stickney off to die and they put water on his head and lugged him home in a hack. they say Bob Carter will lose his place. me and Beany dont know what to do. if we dont tell, Bob will lose his place and if we do we will get licked.

Mar. 12. Mister Stickney is all write today. gosh you bet me and Beany are glad.

Mar. 13 186– brite and fair Mr. Gravel has bought old Heads carrige shop. he is a

45

dandy and wears shiny riding boots and a stove pipe hat and a velvet coat and goes with Dan Ranlet and George Perkins and Johny Gibson and the other dandies. i went down to-day and watched Fatty Walker stripe some wheels.

Mar. 14. clowdy. Elkins and Graves had an oxion to-night. Beany got ten cents for going round town ringing a bell and hollering oxion. i went with Beany and it was lots of fun. Beany wouldent treet. he says he is saving money for something. i know what it is it is a valintine for Lizzie Tole. it was mean of Beany not to treet becaus i did as much hollering as he did.

Mar. 15. The funniest thing hapened to-day you ever saw. after brekfast me and father took a walk and then went and set down on the high school steps. father was

46

telling me some of the things he and Gim
Melcher used to do. father must have been
a ripper when he was young. well ennyway
while we was talking old Ike Shute came
along through the school yard. Ike wears
specks and always carries a little basket on
his arm. he cant see very well, and father
said to me, now you jest keep still and you
will see some fun and when Ike came along
father changed his voice so that it sounded
awfully growly and said where in the devil
are you going with that basket, and Ike was
scart most to deth and said only a little way
down here sir and father said, move on sir
and move dam lively and i nearly died laffing
to see Ike hiper. well after a while i see
Ike coming back with old Swane and old
Kize the policemen. i tell you i was scart
but father only laffed and said you keep still

and i will fix it all right. so when they came up he said to old Kize what is the trouble Filander and he said Mr. Shute here has been thretened by some drunken rascal, and father looked aufully surprised and said that is an infernal shame, when did it happen Isak, and Ike said about fifteen minits ago and father said we have been here about as long as that and i dident see the scoundrel. how did he look Isak, and Ike said i coodent see him very well George but he was a big man and he had a awful deep voice and father said did he stagger enny and Ike said i coodent see wether he did or not but i cood tell he was drunk by his voice. so old Swain and old Kize went down behind the schoolhouse and off thru the carrige shop yard to see if they cood find him, and me and father walked home with Ike to protect him and

48

father said now Isak if ennyone insults you
again jest come to me and if i can catch him i
will break every bone in his body, and father
and Ike shook hands and Ike shook hands
with me and then we went home and father
began to laff and laffed all the way home
and then he told mother and aunt Sarah and
they said it was a shame to play such a trick
upon him and father laffed all the more and
said Ike hadent had so much exercise for a
year and it wood do him good and give him
something to think about. ennyway they
said it was a shame to teech me such things,
and father said he would rather i wood be
tuf than be like Ike, and Aunt Sarah said i
never wood be half as good as Ike for he
never did a wrong thing in his life, and
father laffed and said he dident dass to for
his mother wood shet him in the closet. it

was aufully funny, but i gess they was right. i shall never be half as good as Ike. i wonder if old Swane and old Kize have caught that man yet.

Mar. 16. Pewt dreened 18 marbles and 2 chinees out of me to-day. we was playing first in a hole. school today. sailed boats in the brook in J. Arthur Foster's garden and got pretty wet.

Mar. 17. Scott Briggam has got some little flying squirrels. he is going to get me one for thirty-five cents. i am going to take it out of my cornet money.

Mar. 18. Father wont let me play marbles in ernest. it aint enny fun dreening a feller and then giving them back. i bet father didnt when he was a boy.

Mar. 19. Scott Briggam brought my squirrel today and i paid him 85 cents, 3 ten cents scrips and five cents. i have got it in a bird cage.

Mar. 20. my squirrel got out of the cage last nite and father found him in the water pail drownded. father got up in the night and got a dipper and drank some water out of that pail. he dident eat any brekfast because he was thinking that the squirrel might have been in the pail then. i wonder if it was. ennyway 35 cents of my cornet money has gone up.

Mar. 23. school today. went down to Pewts to draw pictures. Charlie Woodbury can draw the best, then Pewt. and then me. Beany dont like to draw. we was talking about what we was going to be when we grew up. Charlie Woodbury is going to be a picture painter, Pewt is going to be a lawyer, Potter Gorham and Chick Chickering

are going to stuff birds for a living, Beany is
going to be a hack driver, Gim Wingit is
going to run a newspaper, Cawcaw Harding
is going to be a piscopal minister becaus he
says they only have to read their speaches
out of a book, Nipper Brown is going to be
a professor, Priscilla Hobbs is going to play
a organ in the baptist church. Prisil can
play 3 tunes now on a little organ. i am
going to be a cornet player like Bruce Briggam. cornet players can go to all the dances
and fairs and prosessions and are invited in
and treated when people are married and
they serrinade them at night, and they don't
have to work either.

Mar. 25. almost as warm as summer, went
to church and sunday school. Beany has got
a job blowing the organ for Kate Wells. he
only let the wind go out 2 times today. it

was funny becaus when the organ stopped
Mister Wood who was singing let out an
auful hoot before he knowed what he was
doing Beany will lose his job if he does it
again.

Mar. 29, 186– The toads has come out.
fine warm day. me and Potter Gorham have
been ketching toads this afternoon. they sit
in the puddles and peep. folks think it is
frogs but most of it is toads. Potter got 23
and i got 18. tonite i put my toads in a box
in the kitchen after the folks went to bed. in
the night they all got out of the box and
began to hop round and peep mother heard
it and waked father and they lissened. when
i waked up father was coming threw my
room with a big cane and a little tin lamp.
he had put on his britches and was in his
shirt tale, and i said, what are you going to

lick me for now i havent done nothing and he said, keep still there is some one down stairs and mother said dont go down George and father said, lissen i can hear him giving a whistle for his confedrit, i will jump in and give him a whack on the cokonut. i had forgot all about the toads and you bet i was scart. well father he crep down easy and blowed out his lite and opened the door quick and jest lammed round with his club. then i heard him say what in hell have i stepped on, bring a lite here. then i thought of the toads and you bet i was scarter than before, mother went down with a lite and then i heard him say, i will be cussed the whole place is full of toads. then mother said did you ever, and father said he never did, and it was some more of that dam boys works and he yelled upstairs for me to come down and ketch them. so i went down and caught them and put them out all but 2 that father had stepped on and they had to be swep up. then all the folks came down in their nite-gounds and i went up stairs lively and got into bed and pulled the clothes round me tite, but it dident do enny good for father came up and licked me. he dident lick me very hard becaus i gess he was glad it wasent a berglar and if it hadent been for me it might have been berglars insted of toads.

Mar. 30. brite and fair. went out with Potter Gorham. saw some toads 2 robins and a blewbird. gosh it makes a feller feel good to see birds and toads and live things.

Mar. 31. April fool day tomorrow. i am laying for Beany. old Francis licked 5 fellers today becaus they sung rong when we was singing speek kindly it is better far to rule by luv than feer.　　**55**

The Real Diary

April 1. auful cold and rainy. i was going to wright a love letter to Beany and sine Lizzie Toles name to it but i told father about it for fun and he said that it was fourgery and that i cood be prostecuted and sent to jale. so i dident. tonite me and Beany rung five door bells for april fool.

April 2. been trying to get rid of some warts. Pewt says if you hook a piece of pork after dark, rub it on the warts and say arum erum irum orum urum and nurum 3 times turn round twice and throw the pork thru a window, then the warts will all be gone the next day. me and Beany is going to try it tomorrow.

April 3. brite and fair. dident get a chance to hook the pork.

April 4. The band played in the band room to nite. it was warm enuf to have the

56

windows open and we cood hear it. i sat out in the school yard til 10 oclock to hear it and father came out and walked me home. Beany was mad becaus i cared more for the band than for getting rid of the warts.

April 6. dident wright anything last nite, was too scart. i never was so scart in all my life before. me and Beany came awful near getting in jale. we dident know where to hook the pork. i went to our cellar but father was down there making vinigar all the evening, then we went to Beanys cellar but Mister Watson was sitting on the cellar door. so Beany told his father that a man was looking for him to see about a horse and Mister Watson started down to the club stable. then Beany hooked the pork and rubbed it over his warts and then i rubbed it over my warts and we said arum erum

57

irum orum urum and nurum 3 times jest as
Pewt said, turned round twice and i plugged
the pork right threw a gaslite jest then the
gasman came along, he yelled at us and
jumped out of his wagon and went for us.
we ran down threw the school yard as fast
as we cood hiper. there is a hollow in the
corner of the school yard by Bill Morrills
back yard and there is a little hole in the
bottom of the fence where the fellers crawl
threw when the football goes into his garden. we skinned threw that hole jest in
time. the gasman tried to crawl threw but
he coodent, then he clim the high fence but
while he was doing that we ran across the
carrige factory yard and down by the old
brewery up Bow street and home. i went to
bed pretty lively and so did Beany. gosh
but we was scart.

58

April 7. One of Beanys warts has gone.

April 8. brite and fair. my warts have not gone.

April 9. brite and fair. my warts have not gone.

April 10. Clowdy but no rane. my warts have not gone.

April 11. rany. i have got 2 more warts. i gess i hadent ought to have broke that gaslite.

April 12. i have got another.

April 13. bully day. me and Potter Gorham and Chick Chickering went out after toads today. i got 14 but i dident take them home you bet.

April 15. Brite and fair. we all went to church today to see the Lanes. they come from New York and when they go to church everybody goes to see them. there was a

59

boy with them named Willie. i bet i cood lick him.

April 16. Nothing particular today. dont feel very well, kind of headaky and backaky.

April 20. have been sick for 4 days. went to school monday and had to come home. when i got home i fell down on the steps and mother and aunt Sarah came out and got me in the house and put water on my head and rubbed my hands, and then the Docter came and said, well Joanna, children are a good deel of truble and then he felt of my rist and said hum, and then he looked at my tung and said hum again, and then he pride open my mouth and looked down my throte and said hum, and then he pulled off my close and looked me over rite before mother and aunt Sarah and said well he aint

spekled eny. then he said what have you
given him Joanna and mother said, nothing,
and the docter said, all right give him some
more, and mother said i havent given him
enything docter, and then he walked around
the room and picked up some things and
looked at them and then he gave me some of
the wirst tasting stuff i ever took. then he
said i gess he will be better tomorrow, and
then he looked at some more things and
went home. i dident sleep very well that
nite but was auful hot and my head aked
fearful. mother was in my room every time
i waked up, and Sarah too. next day i had
the docter again he looked at some pictures
and things and told mother to give me
some more. i always feel better when the
docter comes in. he dont scare a feller to
deth.

The Real Diary

Well the next day i felt a little better and tried to sit up and have my britches on, but i had to lay down again my head aked so, and after awhile my head felt better and as i laid there i could look out of the window and it seamed as if little chains that you could see through like glass, were floating up and down, they were about an inch long. well i wached them till i almost went to sleep and jest as i was most asleep i heard Beany out in the street holler, say Pewt, did you know that Plupy is going to die, and Pewt said course i did, why dont you tell me some news, and Beany said i heard he swalowed a peech stone and Pewt said it was liver complaint, and then i heard some one say, you boys shet up.

Gosh you bet i was scart. i hadent thought of dying. i began to howl and holler for

mother. she came running in and i told her
i was going to die and i told her about break-
ing the gaslite and a lot of other things and
she told me the docter said i was getting
better and i wood sit up tomorrow. well i
felt better then and wished i hadent told
mother about the gaslite becaus i knew she
wood make me tell father. well mother set
by my bed all the afternoon and read me
some out of Billy Bolegs, jest think of her
doing that, so when supper time came i et a
lettle tost and had some current jelly. when
father come home mother told him about the
gaslite and all he said was i wood have to
pay for it out of my cornet money. i thought
he wood keep me in for a month. i gess
mother must have talked to him.

that nite father slep on a lounge in my
room. i went to sleep most as soon as he

come in. after awhile i dremp i was tied on a sawlog jest going nearer and nearer to the saw and the saw was a going skratch-zoo, skratch-zoo, skratch-zoo. well i tride to pull away but i coodent move and i tride to holler and i coodent make a yip, and jest before the saw sawed into me i woke up. gosh you bet i was glad, but the funny part was that i cood hear the saw going skratch-zoo, skratch-zoo, skratch-zoo, and what do you think it was. it was father snoaring. gosh you ought to have heard him. well at first i laffed, but by and by i wanted to go to sleep and father snoaring so loud i coodent till mother came in and told him to go to bed and she laid on the sofa all nite. the next day i set up and had my britches on and set up to the window all day. i saw Beany and Pewt and i

nocked on the window and waved my claw
at them. i am going out tomorrow.

April 22. i went out today. it was real
warm. i dident go to church becaus i had
been sick. i let my rooster out to fite J.
Arthur Foster's. they were fiting good when
i looked up and there was father looking
over the fence. he made me stop the fite and
shet my rooster up. i wonder if he wood
have stoped them if i hadent been there.
i got 2 eggs today, the old brama that i
swaped for with Ed Tole and a bolten gray
that John Adams give me.

April 23. i went to school today. i dident
have to resite becaus i had been sick. if i
dont get wirse i can go to Mis Packerds
concert tomorow. hope it wont rane.

April 24. brite and fair and it dident

rane tonite, so i went to the concert. all the girls was flowers. Keene was a crocuss and had to come out and sing first becaus the crocuss is the first flower that comes out. she sung i am the first of all the flowers to greet the eyes of spring.

Jenny Morison was a tuch me not and set in the top of a rock and sung tuch me not, tuch me not let me alone. Nell Tole was a piny or a sunflower i have forgot whitch. Jenny Morison and Keene and Nell Tole are the best singers for their size in town. father thinks Keene can sing the best. he feels pretty big about Keene. i told him so one day and he said he had to becaus i dident amount to anything. i think Jenny Morison can sing the best but dont tell him so for he wood give me a bat.

April 25, 186– Cant go down town for a

week because i sassed J. Arthur Foster, that
is J. Arthur Foster says i sassed him but i
dident. Beany had been working for J.
Arthur raking up leaves in his garden. J.
Arthur was a going to give him 10 cents for
it and me and Beany was a going to divide
up on goozeberries and juju paist, but Beany
dident dass to ask J. Arthur for his pay because he had raked all the leaves under J.
Arthurs front steps and he was afraid J.
Arthur wood find out about it and not pay
him. Beany wanted me to ask him but i
dident dass to because i let my rooster out
to fite J. Arthurs last sunday and J. Arthur
dont beleeve in fiting roosters. last night he
was setting on his steps with some company
and he had on his best lavender britches and
his best blew coat.

So Beany said, tell you what Plupy, you

set on your steps and i will set on my steps
and we will holler across the street about
the money that J. Arthur owes me. So Beany
he went across the street to his steps and he
hollered over, hi there Plupy have you got
any chink, and i hollered back, no Beany i
havent got a cent, and Beany he hollered i
shood have 10 cents if J. Arthur Foster
wood pay me what he owes me, and i hollered why in time dont he pay you, and
Beany hollered i gess he hasent got any
chink, and i hollered he has probably spent
all his chink in buying them lavender
britches, and Beany he hollered, well if J.
Arthur Foster needs the money more than i
do he can have it. well while we was hollering mister Head and the Head girls who
was setting on their steps got up and went
into the house laffing, and the company at

68

J. Arthurs all laffed, and J. Arthur came
down and beckoned to Beany and Beany
he went running over to get his 10 cents
and J. Arthur he said, Elbridge, that is
Beanys name, Elbridge you cood have your
money enny time if you had asked me for
it decently, but now i shall not pay you for
a week and i shall not imploy you enny
more. Tell you what, Beany came over to my
steps feeling pretty cheap and we was talking about it when mother called me in and
sent me up stairs, and said she wood tell
father as soon as he came home. So i went
up stairs and looked out of the window jest
in time to see Beany's father lugging Beany
in by the neck. Well that nite after father
got home he jawed me and said i coodent go
down town for a week and made me go to
J. Arthurs right before the company and ask

his forgiveness, and Beany had to to. J. Arthur was a pretty good fellow and said it was all right, and dident want our fathers not to let us go down town, but father said i must learn to be respectable to my elders. Gosh we dident know J. Arthur was a elder. We knowed elder Stevens and elder Stewart and deacon Gooch and we always was respectable to them, and if we had knowed that J. Arthur Foster was a elder we woodent have sassed him for nothing.

April 26. Yesterday and day before it was brite and fair, and yesterday was as warm as summer. today it was cold and it snowed a little, jest enuf to make the ground look as if it was covered with salt. the birds looked all humped up. i bet the frogs hind legs is about froze. it is raining now. if i was a frog i woodent come out of the mud until summer. perhaps they cant stay under more than six months.

April 27. Warm again. 2 eggs today. i have got another hen. Willyam Perry Molton gave it to me. it is a leghorn and his other hens licked it and made its comb bludy and so he gave it to me. it was on the nest today but did not lay. i went to church. Mr. Cram preeched. he talked all about birds and flowers and i liked it.

April 28. brite and fair. all 3 hens were on the nest but dident lay.

April 29. no eggs today. mother said the hens cakled all the morning. brite and fair.

April 30. i dont see what the mater is with my hens. i havent got 1 egg this week. father said there was a rat in the koop. i got a steel trap of Sam Diar and tonite i set it in the koop. i put a peace of cheeze on it. tomorow morning i gess mister rat wont steal any more eggs.

May 1. what do you think. this morning i got up to get my rat and i found that my best hen, the bolton gray that John Adams gave me had tried to pick the cheeze out of the trap and the trap had caught her by the neck and killed her. i felt most bad enuf to cry. i thought i cood get up before the hen did. i went to the may brekfast today. it was mayfair day and they had a brekfast. me and Pewt, Beany, Whacker and Pozzy Chadwick, Micky Gould, Pop Clark, Prisilla Hobbs, Chick Chickering, Potter Gorham, Pile Wood, Curly Conner and all the fellers were there. we had a good time and et till just before school time and we had to hiper so as not to be late.

May 2. no eggs today. both hens went on the nest. i am going to lay for that rat with my bowgun.

May 3. what do you think. this noon i set in the hen koop 1 hour. the brama went on the nest and set a while and came off and cakled. then i looked and she had lade an egg. i left the egg there and hid behind a barrel and got my bowgun ready for the rat. well the leghorn hen went on the nest and i suposed she was a going to lay, but she broke rite into that egg and began to gobble it up. i was so mad that i let ding at her with the bowgun and just then she stuck up her head and the arrow took her rite in the back of the head. well i wish you cood have seen her. she hollered one little pip and then went rite out of the nest backwards and flapped round awful. i picked

73

her up and she was dead. i dident mean
to kill her, i only wanted to make her jump
and learn her not to eat eggs. O dear, i
dont know what father will say when he
finds it out.

May 5, 186– Saw a bully fite today. Cris
Staples and Charlie Foster. Charlie is visiting his uncle J. Arthur Foster, the feller
that we sassed. that is he said we did but
we dident. Charlie is a city feller, he lives
in Chelsy and thinks he knows a pile about
things and gets mad if we call him names.
now every feller who amounts to anything
has a nickname, and some of them have 2
or 3. my nicknames are Plupy and Skinny
and Polelegs, and Beany is called Bullet-
head and sometimes Fatty. i told Charlie
that if i called him Charlie the fellers would
call him sissy or Mary and he better agree

to let me call him bulldog or tomcat or
diddly or gobbler or some nickname whitch
wood mean something. but he said he would
lam the head off of enny feller which called
him names.

well you jest see what trouble he got into
for not having a nickname. he would have
knowed better than that if he hadent lived
in Chelsy.

Well today me and Charlie was setting on
his steps. Beany was mad because i was
going with Charlie and he had gone riding
with his father, and he felt pretty big because his father let him drive. well while
we were setting there along came Cris
Staples who carries papers for Lane and
Rollins store, and Cris hollered over, hullo
Polelegs. Charlie hadent heard enyone call
me Polelegs. and i said, i woodent stand that

75

if i was you Charlie, now less see you lam
the head off of him, and Charlie he started
across the road and walked up to Cris and
said who in time are you calling Polelegs
and Cris wasent going to back down and
said, you, and Charlie said jest drop them
papers and i will nock your face rite off,
and Cris dropped his papers and they went
at it. it was the best fite i have seen this
year. they fit from Mr. Head's down to Gim
Ellisons corner, and Cris licked time out of
Cnarlie, and Charlie began to yell and give
up and then Cris let go of his hair and told
him he was too smart, and that it was me
he was calling Polelegs and not him, and he
better not be as smart another time, and Cris
he picked up his papers and went off with a
great slit in his jacket and his necktie way
round on one side, and Charlie came home

76

howling and Aunt Foster, Charlie's grand-
mother came out and said, that is what you
get Charlie for quareling. see how much
better Harry feels, and i said, yes mam.
Charlie is never going to speak to me
again.

May 7. Beany was pretty mad when I
told him about the fite becaus he dident see
it. i gess he will find it don't pay to get
mad with me. i saw Charlie today but he
dident speak. he has got a black eye. Cris
has got a funny looking nose on one side.

May 8. Chitter Robinson went in swiming today. i bet it was cold.

May 9. Went down to the high school
yard tonite to hear the band play. they have
got a new leader a Mister Ashman of Boston. he can play a cornet with 1 hand. i
went down today to pay the gasman for the

gaslite i broke. it cost 1 dollar and i have only got 87 cents for my cornet. sometimes i dont believe i shall ever get that cornet. Scott Brigam can blow a bugle. a bugle is like a cornet only a cornet has 3 keys and a bugle is all covered with flappers and curly things where you put your fingers. Rashe Belnap can play a cornet splendid but he dont play very often. Frank Hirvey plays one that goes over his shoulder way behind his back. gosh i wish i cood get a cornet.

May 10. father has found out about my killing that hen. he dident get mad but said i ought to have cut her head off and she wood be good to eat, but i supose it is too late now for it is almost a week ago and i burried her the next day.

May 11. me and Potter Gorham went mayflowering today. i got a bunch and sold

78

them to a student named Chizzum for 35 cents. i put it with my cornet money. i have now got $1.22. i can get a cornet for 25 dollars a second hand one. i am afraid i shall never get that cornet.

May 12. Rany last nite and this morning. in the afternoon it cleared up. gosh i wish you cood have seen the licking Beany got tonite. me and Beany went out to go up to see Pewt and make some sweet fern sigars. Beany came over for me and went up to Pewts. on the way Beany went up and rung his doorbell and we hid behind the fence and Mister Watson, Beany's father, came out holding a light and shading it with his hand. the wind blew the lite out and in going in again he hit his head an awful bump against the door. me and Beany nearly died laffing only we tride not to laff

79

too loud. well we went up to Pewts and Pewt had been sent to bed for something and so we started back and met a man who said is this you Elbridge, it was pretty dark and Beany said yes and Mister Watson grabbed us both by the collar and said, so you are the boys who rung my doorbell and then he give Beany a rap on the side of the head and began to shake him round lively and while he was shaking Beany up i put for home. i hid behind the fence and i cood hear him say i will learn you to asosiate with that misable Shute boy and wast your time ringing doorbells, and Beany was saying, o father i will never do it again. i nearly died laffing to hear Beany a rattling round on the sidewalk. i hope Mister Watson wont tell father. i gess he wont for he gets over his mad pretty quick. every time

80

i think of Beanys legs flying round in the air i giggle rite out and when i think of Mister Watson bumping his head i nearly die. sometimes i think it pays to be tuff.

May 13 186– Keene and Cele have got some new crokay slippers. you bet they feel pretty big about it.

May 14. nothing particular today.

May 15. Went in swimming today. the water was pretty cold but i swum acros the river twise.

May 16. the suckers have come. Potter Gorham caught three yesterday. me and Potter was going yesterday after school but father woodent let me becaus i dident split my kindlings.

May 17. the band played tonight. father made me go to bed at nine but i cood hear it becaus my window is jest acros the road.

they are playing a new peace. it is the woodup quickstep, they say Ned Kendall cood play it on a bugle better than ennybody. old Robinson cood and Mister Ashman can play it splendid. it goes

> ta-ta tata, ta-ta tata, ta-ta tata
> tatatatatatata.
> ta-te-ta-te-tiddle iddle-a
> ta-te-ta-te-tiddle-iddle-a
> ta-te-ta-te-tiddle-iddle-a
> tiddle-iddle-iddle-iddle-ata

it is the best peace they play exept departed days. that always makes me feel like crying it is kinder sad like. i hope i can get my cornet some day.

May 19. had a auful toothake today and had to go down to docter Pitman and he pulled it out. i tell you it hurt. Docter

82

Pitman said the roots must have reached
way to the back of my neck. Beany went
with me and then told all round that i hollered. you jest wait Beany.

May 21. erly this afternoon me and Fatty
Melcher got some real segars at Henry Sim-
sons store and went down behind old man
Churchills store and smoked them. we were
both auful sick and laid there all the afternoon. when i went home i walked wobbly
and mother asked me if i was sick and she
put me to bed and was going to send for
the docter, but father came in and when he
found out what aled me he laffed and said
it served me rite. then after supper he set
out on the steps rite under my window and
smoked a old pipe and i cood smell it and
i thought i shood die. then mother asked
him to go away and he laffed and said all

rite, but he gessed i had enuf for one day and she said she gessed so and i gess so too. he said if it hadent made me sick he wood have licked me.

i dont see why it is so, father swears sometimes when he hits his thum with a hammer and once when he was in the dark he was walking towards the door with his arms out to feel for the door, one arm went on one side of the door and the other arm on the other side and he hit his nose a fearful bump rite on the ege of the door, and i wish you cood have heard him swear, well if i swear he licks me, and he smokes and if i do he says he will lick me and he dont go to church and if i dont go he says he will lick me. O dear i gess i wont smoke enny more.

84

May 22. Went in swimming today twise, once down to the raceway and once up to the gravel.

May 23. Went butterflying with Chick Chickering today, it is a little early for them, but we got two blew and black ones and three little red ones. Me and Chick are making aquariams. Chick has got a splendid glass one. i made mine out of a butter firkin. i sawed it off half way and then washed it out with soft soap and rensed it 2 or 3 times and then i put in some white sand and stones and i have got some little minnies and kivies and a little pickerel. it looks splendid and i change the water every 3 days.

May 24. Nothing particular today.

May 25. i can swim under water from the big tree on Moulton's side of the river at the gravel to the tree on the bank on Gilman's side. i went in 3 times today.

May 26. My rooster is sick. i gess he has et something. he sits all humped up. i went in swimming 2 times today.

May 27. My rooster is pretty sick. i tride to give him some kiann pepper tonite. father said kiann pepper was good for sick hens, so i held his mouth open and give him a spoonful. when i let him go he kept his mouth open and sorter sneezed pip-craw pip-craw pip-craw, and then he went to the water dish and began to drink. i think he is better because he hadent drank any water for 2 days before. he was still drinking when i went away. i gess he will be a lot better tomorrow.

May 28. What do you think, this morning when i went out to feed my hens i found my rooster dead. he had drank up all the water and he was all puffed up. i felt pretty bad. father says i gave him enuf kiann pepper for a horse. he aught to have told me. he was a pretty good rooster too. i am having pretty tuff luck.

May 29. i read over my diary today. i have forgot to tell whether it was brite and fair or rany, i can't say now.

May 30, 186– Nothing particular today. brite and fair.

May 31. brite and fair. went up to Whacker Chadwicks today after school to help him plant his garden. we had about a bushel of potatoes to plant and it was fun to sit round a basket and cut up the potatoes. after a while Gim Erly and Luke Mannux cume along and we began to plug potatoes at them, they plugged them back and we

had a splendid fite, me and Whack and
Pozzy and Boog Chadwick on one side and
Gim Erly and Luke Mannux and Bob Ridly
on the other. Luke Mannux hit me twice
rite in the back of the head. i am going up
tomorrow to help them some more. went in
swimming once today.

May 32 no i ment June 1. i went up
to Chadwicks after school. Captin Chadwick was there and they wasent enny plug-
gin potatoes. went in swimming.

June 2. Rany. Beany is mad with me. i
dont care.

June 3. went to church today.

June 4. clowdy but no rane. went up to
Chadwicks today and sawed wood. Boog
and Pozzy fit while me and Whack sawed
wood then we went in swiming down to
Sandy Bottom. some body tide some hard

88

gnots in my shirt. i forgot to split my kind-lings tonite.

June 5. brite and fair. Beany is still mad.

June 6. brite and fair. i know what Beany is mad about. he thinks i told about his getting a licking. i dident tell. he can stay mad if he wants to.

June 7. father has bought a horse of Dan Randlet. i rode up to Brentwood with Sam Diar to get it. it is the prettiest horse i ever saw. i rode it down from Brentwood and it goes jest as easy as sitting on a spring board. when i got home Beany got over his mad and came over and i gave him a ride. me and Beany never were mad so long before.

June 9. Rany. this afternoon me and Beany and father went to ride with the new horse. her name is Nellie.

June 10. brite and fair. we keep Nellie

down to Jo Hanes stable. Frank Hanes is learning me how to clean her off. she nipped my arm today and made a black and blew spot. went in swimming today.

i have to get up every morning and harnes Nelly and drive father to the depot. i like it because i always race with the men coming down front street. there is George Dergin and Fred Sellivan and Gim Wingit and i can beat them all. i dont tell father that i race. i rode Nellie this afternoon with Frank Hanes and Ed Tole. i dident go in swimming to-day.

June 11. brite and fair. Nellie kicked me today. i gess i scrached her today too hard with the curycomb. it dident hurt me much. i went in swimming twise.

June 12. brite and fair. Me and Chick Chickering went bullfroging today, we got 3

90

dozen hind legs and sold them to Mr. Hirvey for 30 cents and took our pay in icecream.

June 13. Rode Nellie this noon. i have to go to the half past five train every nite for father. i like to drive but i dont like to go every nite.

June 14. Rashe Belnap and Horris Cobbs go in swimming every morning at six o'clock. i got a licking today that beat the one Beany got. last summer me and Tomtit Tomson and Cawcaw Harding and Whack and Poz and Boog Chadwick went in swimming in May and all thru the summer until October. one day i went in 10 times. well i dident say anything about it to father so as not to scare him. well today he dident go to Boston and he said i am going to teech you to swim. when i was as old as you i cood swim said he, and you

91

must lern, i said i have been wanting to lern to swim, for all the other boys can swim. so we went down to the gravil and i peeled off my close and got ready. now said he, you jest wade in up to your waste and squat down and duck your head under. i said the water will get in my nose. he said no it wont jest squat rite down. i cood see him laffin when he thought i wood snort and sputter.

so i waded out a little ways and then div in and swam under water most across, and when i came up i looked to see if father was supprised. gosh you aught to have seen him. he had pulled off his coat and vest and there he stood up to his waste in the water with his eyes jest bugging rite out as big as hens eggs, and he was jest a going to dive for my dead body. then

92

i turned over on my back and waved my hand at him. he dident say anything for a minute, only he drawed in a long breth. then he began to look foolish, and then mad, and then he turned and started to slosh back to the bank where he slipped and went in all over. When he got to the bank he was pretty mad and yelled for me to come out. when i came out he cut a stick and whaled me, and as soon as i got home he sent me to bed for lying, but i gess he was mad becaus i about scart the life out of him. but that nite i heard him telling mother about it and he said that he div 3 times for me in about thirty feet of water. but he braged about my swiming and said i cood swim like a striped frog. i shall never forget how his boots went kerslosh kerslosh kerslosh when we were skinning home thru croslots.

i shall never forget how that old stick hurt either. ennyhow he dident say ennything about not going in again, so i gess i am all rite.

June 15, 186– Johnny Heeld, a student, came to me and wanted me to carry some tickets to a dance round to the girls in the town. there was about 1 hundred of them. he read the names over to me and i said i knew them all. so after school me and Beany started out and walked all over town and give out the tickets. i had a long string of names and every time i wood leave one i wood mark out the name. i dident give the Head girls any because they told father about some things that me and Beany and Pewt did and the Parmer girls and the Cilley girls lived way up on the plains and i dident want to walk up there, so when

94

i went over to Hemlock side to give one, i
went over to the factory boarding house and
give some to them. they was auful glad
to get them too and said they would go to
the dance. some people was not at home
and so i gave their tickets to the next house.
it took me till 8 o'clock and i got 1 dollar
for it. i dont beleive those girls that dident
get their tickets will care much about going
ennyway. i gess the Head girls wont want
to tell on me another time.

June 16. Dennis Cokely and Tomtit Tomson had a fite behind Hirvey's resterent today. Hirvey stopped them jest as they were
having a good one. Thats jest the way. i
dont see why they always want to stop a fite.
All fellers fite for is to see which can lick,
and how can they tell unless they fite it out.

June 17. Brite and fair. They is going to be a big cattle show here this fall. They are going to have it in a field up by the depot. They are going to have horse trots and shows and everything. We are going to have no school. it dont come for an auful while yet. Charles Taylor is going to have Nelly to ride.

June 18. Me and Mickey Gould had a race horseback. he had one of Ben Merril's little black horses. we raced way round Kensington ring. i cood beat trotting and he cood beat running. when i got home Nelly was so swetty that father told me not to ride her for a week.

June 19. Went up to Chadwicks after school. Boog and Whack got Willie fiting with Johnny Rogers. Willie licked him. Willie is Whack's little brother. he is a auful cunning little feller. he can fite too. all the Chadwick's can fite.

June 20. Brite and fair. i am going fishing tonite with Potter Gorham.

June 21. brite and fair. went fishing today with Potter Gorham. i cought 5 pirch and 4 pickeril. i cleaned them and we had them for supper. father said they was the best fish he ever et. i also cought the biggest roach i ever saw, almost as big as a sucker, and i cant tell what i did with him. i thought Potter had hooked him for fun, but he said he dident, and we hunted everywhere for him. i dont know where i put that roach.

June 22. the students had their dance last nite. they had a auful time. some of the girls which dident get no tickets was mad, and the students which wanted them to go

was mad and they went to Johnny Heeld
and give him time. then he went round
and told them how it was and give them
tickets. well the nite of the dance everything was all rite until lots of people came
which hadent been on the list, but which we
had given tickets. well the students dident
want to let them in and they were mad, and
Chick Randal hit a student named Pendry
rite in the nose and nocked his glasses off,
and Nichols nocked Johnny Lord way acros
the entry and they was going to have a
big fite when Bob Carter and 2 or 3 men
stoped it. today Johnny Heeld came down
to the house and said i had got things all
mixed up and father made me give back the
dollar. but he told Johnny Heeld he hadent
ought to have let me try such a hard job.
Gosh, i am glad father thinks it was a mis-

take, and dont know that i did it on purpose.

June 23. there is a dead rat in the wall in my room. it smells auful.

June 24. Rany. most time for vacation. the smell in my room is fearful.

June 25. more trouble today. it seems as if there wasent any use in living. nothing but trouble all the time. mother said i coodent sleep in that room until the rat was taken out. well father he came into my room and sniffed once and said, whew, what a almity smell. then he held his nose and went out and came back with mister Staples the father of the feller that called me Polelegs. well he came in and put his nose up to the wall and sniffed round until he came to where my old close hung. then he said, thunder George, this is the place, rite be-

hind this jacket, it is the wirst smell i ever
smelt. then he threw my close in a corner
and took out his tools and began to dig a
hole in the wall, while father and mother
and aunt Sarah stood looking at him and
holding their nose. after he dug the hole he
reached in but dident find ennything, then
he stuck in his nose and said, it dont smell
enny in there. then they all let go of their
nose and took a sniff and said murder it
is wirse than ever it must be rite in the room
somewhere. then father said to me, look in
those close and see if there is ennything
there. so i looked and found in the poket
of my old jaket that big roach that i lost,
when i went fishing with Potter Gorham. it
was all squashy and smelt auful. father was
mad and made me throw the jaket out of
the window and wont let me go fishing for

100

a week. ennyway i know now what became of my roach.

June 26. Keene and Cele are going to sing in the Unitarial quire. father says he will give them some bronze boots. mother got them some new nets for their hair today. girls has lots more done for them than fellers.

June 27, 186– Brite and fair. school closed today. we dont have enny more school til September. snapcrackers have come. 8 cents a bunch at old Langlys store. Lane and Rollins sell them for 10 cents. torpedos 8 cents a bunch. pin wheels 1 cent each. Pewt is going to have a cannon. father wont let me have a cannon. he says i dont know enny more than to look into it and blow my head off.

June 28. clowdy but no rane. 4th of

July pretty soon. father says when he was a boy all they had for fireworks was balls of wool soked in tirpentine whitch they lit an fired round. i am glad i did not live then.

June 30. clowdy but no rane. went in swimming 3 times today. i am going bullfroging Monday.

June 31. no July 1. Went to church today.

July 2. i went bullfroging today. thunder storm today.

i have got 10 bunches of snapcrackers and some slowmatch. i spent a dolar of my cornet money. i gess i shall never get that cornet. i hope it wont rane the 4th.

July 3. Nite before 4th. Pewt and Beany can stay out all nite. father took my snapcrackers into his room and said if i get up before 5 i cant have enny.

July 4. i am to tired to wright ennything. i never had so much fun in my life.
i only got burned 5 times. 1 snapcracker
went off rite in my face and i coodent see
ennything til mother washed my eyes out.
Zee Smith fired a torpedo and a peace of
it flew rite in the corner of my eye and
made a blew spot there. i fired every one
of my snapcrackers. it took me all day.

July 5. brite and fair. i dident wake up
today til 10 o'clock. i was pretty sore and
my eyes felt as if they was sawdust in
them.

July 6. brite and fair. father staid home
today. i wanted him to go fishing but he
woodent.

July 7. father told me i cood go fishing
and stay all day. i dont know what had
come over him becaus most always he raises

103

time when i go fishing and dont come home
erly. so i went and cought 3 pickerels and
4 pirch and 2 hogbacks and went in swiming 2 times. well as i was a coming home
2 or 3 people met me and said they was
company at my house, so when i got home i
skined in the back way so as not to see
the company til i got on my best britches,
but i met father in the door and he told
me to go rite up to mothers room and see
the company. so i skined up to her room
holding my hand behind me becaus i had
tore my britches auful getting over a fence
and i dident want the company to see. well
what do you think the company was. it was
the homliest baby you ever see, it looked jest
like a munky and made feerful faces and
kinder squeaked like. Mother was sick and

they was a old fat woman who told me to
go out, but mother said she wanted to see
me and she kissed me and asked me to kiss
the baby. i dident want to but i did it becaus mother was sick. mother asked me
how many fish i caught and what kind and
i told her and said she shood have some for
her supper, but she said she gessed she
woodent have enny jest then.

then i went down stairs and father said
did i like the baby and i said it was homly,
and he said it was 10 times as good looking as i was and he said he was glad that
when the baby grode up it woodent have
Beany and Pewt to play with and woodent
be tuff like me, and then Aunt Sarah said
she gessed me and Beany and Pewt wasent
enny tuffer than father and Gim Melcher

were when they was boys, and then father laffed and told me to go to bed and i went. that was a auful homly baby ennyway.

July 8. nothing particular today. you bet that baby can howl. went to church.

July 9. brite and fair. most every morning we go up in mothers room to see the old fat woman wash the baby and hear it howl. it turns black in the face. i bet it will be a fiter.

July 10. i have got a new nickname. it is yallerlegs. that is becaus father bought me a pair of kinder yellow britches, and made me wear them. i bet he woodent like to be called yallerlegs.

July 11. brite and fair. went in swiming today to a new place. we call it the stump. it is up by the eddy.

July 12. a thunder storm. in the after-

106

noon went fishing but dident get a bite.
Pewts father says fish wont bite after a
thunder storm.

July 13. a auful hot day. tonite i went
up to the depot to see Majer Blake and
Charles Tole fite over passengers to the
beach.

July 14. i am going to the beach to stop
with Beany in his fathers tent. it is called
hotel de pig.

July 15. i gess i will go tomorrow.

July 16. me and Beany went to the
beach and stopped all day and all nite. we
had a bully time.

July 17. another hot day. went in swiming 4 times. my back is all burned.

July 18. me and Beany got in the news-
leter today. the paper said the siamese twins
was at the beach stoping at Watsons tent.

Pewt was mad becaus we got in the paper and he dident and told all round that it dident mean me and Beany but Rashe Belnap and Horris Cobbs.

July 19. Hot as time. nothing particular today.

July 20. Hot as time. nothing particular today.

July 21. Auful hot. big thunder shower the litening struck a tree in front of Perry Moltons house.

July 22. Went to church. Beany let the wind out of the organ and it squeaked and made everybody laff. Keene and Cele sing in the quire. father feels pretty big about it.

July 23. i got stung by hornets today. i went in swiming at the eddy and when i was drying my close i set rite down on a stump where there was a nest of yellow bellied hornets. they all lit on me and i thought i was afire for a minit. i ran and div rite off the bank and swam way out under water. when i came up they were buzing round jest where i went down. when i came out the fellers put mud on my bites and after a while they stoped hurting. i tell you the fellers jest died laffing to see me run and holler.

July 24. Brite and fair. i was all sweled up with hornet bites but they dident hurt enny, i looked jest like Beany when he had the mumps. everyone laffed at me.

July 25. i got a fishhook in my leg to-day. me and Fatty Melcher was a fishing when we got our lines tangled. i hollered first cut, but i dident have enny nife and Fatty woodent let me have his nife. So we

109

got jerking our lines kinder mad like and all of a suddin the hook got into my leg. gosh you bet it hurt. me and Fatty got the hook out but it bled some. the worst of it was there was a wirm on the hook and when we got the hook out they wasent enny wirm there. Fatty says people sometimes dies from having wirms in them. i bet this one has crawled way in. it may grow inside of me. something is always hapening to me. when i got home i went down to docter Derborns store and bought some wirm medicine and swalowed sum. it was auful bitter. it cost 20 cents out of my cornet money.

July 26. brite and fair. i was all rite today except my leg was stiff. mother asked what made me lame and she put on a peace of pork. i told her about the wirm and she said the pork wood draw him out if he

110

was there but she gessed he dident go in.
when i told her about the wirm medecine
she jest set down and laffed. so i gess i
needent wory about having wirms. i went
down to doctor Derborns and tride to get
him to take the medicine back but he said
he woodent. i think he is pretty mean not
to.

July 27. i coodent go in swiming today
on account of my leg. all the fellers went
in and i had to set on the bank and see
them.

July 28. Coodent go in swiming today
either. my leg is nearly well. mother took
off the pork today. it was all white where
the pork was. i can go in swiming Monday.
i went down to the library tonite. it is the
first time i have been down since Joe Parsons chased me out. i gess he has forgoten

it. i got out Bush Boys to read. it is a splendid book about shooting lions and zebras and gerafs and everything.

July 29. i tried to have father let me stay away from church today because my leg was sore but he said all rite you can stay, but i gess that leg will be too sore to let you go in swiming this week. so i went to church and dident limp enny. this afternoon i set under the apple tree and read Bush Boys. father and mother went to ride with Nellie. it is the first time mother has been out. Aunt Sarah took care of the baby. they gess they will name it Edward Ashman Shute. i gess it is named Ashman after the leader of the band. i am going to tell him tomorrow and see if he wont sell me a cornet on trust. brite and fair.

July 30. Brite and fair. i told father i

112

was going down to see Mr. Ashman, and he said if you ever do i will lick you. the babys name is Edward Ashton Shute and not Ashman. i woodent name him for enny cornet player. it is pretty tuff luck. if i cood have got that cornet i woodent have minded a licking. went in swiming today.

July 31. Franky had the croop last nite. i waked up and heard him cough auful funny and kinder as if his throte was tite. i called mother and she came in and hollered for Aunt Sarah and father and they rushed round lively and gave him egg and sugar and put hot cloths on his throte till he howled and after he cood howl he was all well. Aunt Sarah took him in with her the rest of the nite. father said i was a brick to wake up and call them. i dont know

113

when he has called me a brick before. went in swiming 3 times to-day.

Aug. 1. brite and fair. Annie tumbled down the front steps from the top to the bottom. she howled and mother thought she was about killed but she was so fat that she dident hurt her.

Aug. 2. father came home early to-day and took mother and Aunt Sarah and Keene & Georgie to ride. Me and Cele staid to look after the house. Cele went up stairs to look after the baby and when she was gone i got Annie and Franky fiting. it was the funniest fite i ever saw. they jest pushed each other round and tried to claw each other. while they was fiting Cele came down stairs and pulled them apart and boxed their ears and made them go in different rooms. She jawed me and said she wood tell father.

114

when father came home she told on me and
father sent me to bed at six o'clock. You
jest wait Cele and you will find out.

Aug. 3, 186– brite and fair. the fellers
played a pretty mean trick on me tonite.
they played it on Nibby Hartwel last nite.
Nibby is visiting his aunt and comes from
the city and is pretty green like most folks
from the city. you see if i hadent got sent
to bed becaus Cele told on me i wood have
been there and seen them play it on Nibby.
well last nite all the fellers was out. Whack
and Boog and Pozzy and Pewt and Beany
and Nipper and Cawcaw and Pile and Chick
and Micky and Pricilla and Fatty. Nibby
he was there too. they wanted to play lead
the old blind horse to water and i was to be
the blind horse. they said they had some
fun playing it the nite before, that was

115

when they played it on Nibby but i dident
know that. Well you blindfole a feller and
give him a rope and a swich and the other
fellers get on the other end of the rope and
the feller nearest you has a bell and rings it
and you pull and if you can pull him up to
you, you can paist time out of him with
your swich, only if you pull off your blindfole all the fellers can paist time out of you.
Well they blindfoled me and hollered ready
and i began to yank and pull and the feller
rung his bell and he came pretty hard at
first but i kept yanking and bimeby he come
so quick that i nearly fell over back wards
and i felt him and grabed him and began to
paist time out of him when he grabed away
my swich and began to paist me, and that
wasent fair and i pulled off my blindfole
and who do you suppose it was, well it was

116

Wiliam Perry Molton and he was mad.
they had tied me to his door bell and i had
yanked out almost ten feet of wire. when i
saw who it was gosh i began to holler and
he stoped licking me. i gess he never
licked anyone before becaus he dident know
jest how to lay it on. well when he found
out how it was he let me go but he said he
shood have to do something about the boys
distirbing him so. it was a pretty mean trick
to play on a feller. we are going to try and
play it on Pop Clark tomorrow nite.

Aug. 4. brite and fair. me and Hiram
Mingo had a race today to see whitch cood
swim the furtherest under water. i beat him
easy. he can lick me but i can beat him
swiming.

Aug. 5. Nothing particular today. only
church.

117

Aug. 6. the baby was sick today. had the doctor.

Aug. 7. the baby was sicker. i dident go in swiming.

Aug. 8. the baby is better today. i went in swiming 5 times.

Aug. 9. Raned all day. The baby is all rite. i went bullfroging with Chick Chickering.

Aug. 10. Nellie is sick. Joe Hanes cut a hole in her and put in a onion and some braded hair and then father took her out to pastur. i cant ride her for a month.

Aug. 11. brite and fair. mister Watson, Beanys father got throwed off of his horse today and renched his rist. the horse coodent have throwed him but the gert broke. Mister Watson can ride splendid.

118

Aug. 12. brite and fair. No more church this month. bully.

Aug. 13. brite and fair. i went down to Ed Toles and me and Ed rode on the hack with Joe Parmer.

Aug. 14. Ed Tole and Frank Hanes are mad. Frank hollered over to Ed, Ed Tole fell in a hole and coodent get out to save his sole, and Ed hollered back Frank Hanes aint got no branes. and then they was mad.

Aug. 15. Wiliam Perry Molton has got some ripe apples in his back yard. me and Pewt helped him ketch some hens today and he said we cood have some apples if they was any on the ground. they was only 2 wirmy ones but before we left 5 or 6 fell off. i gess it was becaus Pewt pushed me agenst the tree. they was pretty good apples too.

Aug. 16. Rany. i went fishing with Potter Gorham. caught 3 roach and 5 hornpowt. we et them for supper. father said i can clean fish most as well as he can. he says he will come home some day erly and go a fishing.

Aug. 17. John Gardner has hung up a Grant and Colfax flag. they will be some fun this fall.

Aug. 18. brite and fair. Today i went fishing with Fatty Melcher. we caught some ells and some hornpowt. ells and hornpowt can live a long time out of water and so when i got home i put 5 that were alive in the rane water barril.

Aug. 19. brite and fare. it is fun to sit round all day sunday and not have to go to church.

Aug. 20. brite and fair. i had to spend the whole morning in going to the river for

water for washing. it was wash day and
when mother went to the rane water barril
there was 5 dead hornpowt floting on the
top. she made me tip the barrel over and
get water from the river. they was some
fun for Beany helped me and he stood in the
hand cart and filled the tubs and all of a.
sudden i let go and the old cart flew up and
Beany and the tub and the pail and everything went rite in. Beany isent going to
speak to me ever again.

Aug. 21, 186– Gosh, we are having fun
now. what do you think. they is going to
be a big mass meeting this fall. Ben Butler
and Jake Ely and lots of old pelters are
going to be here, and they is going to be 4
or 5 bands and lots of fun. well before that
comes they is going to be lots of political
meetings and the first one is to be next week,

and father is going to make a speach. Gim
Luverin and Bil Morrill and General Mars-
ten and Tom Levitt, and he is a ripper to
holler. and they want father to make a
speach. father says he must work for the
party and perhaps he can get his salery
rased. so he has been a riting every nite
and mumbling it over to hisself and last nite
he said he had got it. tonite he is a going
to speak it to us.

Aug. 22. last nite father studed his
speach over and let us stay up to hear it.
he stood up and looked auful stirn and
put one hand in the buzum of his shert. i
coodent help laffin, but he told me to shet
up or i cood go to bed and so i shet up. i
tell you it was fine. It begun Mister Mod-
dirator had i suposed, or for 1 moment dremp
that i a humble offis holder under this glori-

ous government, wood have been called upon
to speak, i shood have remained at home
with my wife and my children.

i said, if you dont want to make a speach
why dont you stay at home that nite, and he
said 1 more word from you sir and you go to
bed. so i dident yip again.

then he went on like this, were it not that
a crool axident in my erly youth, in my far
away boyhood days prevented me from vol-
untearing and desecrating my life to my
country's welfare, in the strugle jest ended i
wood have poared out evry drop of my blud
to have maintained her owner and the owner
of her flag. mother began to laff and said
George how can you tell such feerful stories,
you know you were scart most to deth because you was afraid you wood be drafted.

father said they was a lot of old fellows

traveling round the country and talking that way who coodent have been drug into the war with a ox chane. then he stood on the other leg a while and said, it is peculiarly aproprate that Exeter, the berth place of Lewis Cas, the educater of Webster, the home of Amos Tuck, of General Marston shood be fourmost in the party strife, and as for me i wirk only for my partys good, my countrys good, without feer or hope of reward. they was a lot more to it, and some of it you cood hear about a mile he hollered so.

Aug. 23. We are all going the nite of the rally. mother says she wont go for she wood be ashamed to hear father tell such dredful stories. Aunt Sarah dont want to go because she is afraid father will brake down. but she has got to go with me and Keene and Cele and Georgie.

124

Aug. 24. father practised his speach tonite and we all hollered and claped at the fine parts. he has got a new pair of boots. they hurt like time and he only wears them nites when he is practising his speach.

Aug. 25. father licked me tonite becaus i spoke some of his speach to Beany. he was auful mad and said i was the bigest fool he ever see. the fellers have got up a Grant Club. Pricilla cant belong becaus he is a demicrat.

Aug. 26. father called me and Beany out behind the barn tonite and gave us 10 cents apeace if we woodent say enything about his speach. after supper father practised again but he dident holler so loud becaus he was afraid some body wood hear him and mother dident want him to wake up the baby, and it was sunday too.

125

Aug. 27. it has been brite and fair all the week and hot as time. i have to go to the river for soft water because it hasent raned eny since i had to tip over the rane water barril. i have got a little tirtle as big as a cent. father went down to General Marstons office tonite to arrange about the rally. he came home and practised about an hour. i gess he wood have practised all nite if the baby hadent waked up and hollered.

Aug. 28. we are all getting ready for the rally. Keene and Cele and Georgie have got some new plad dresses. father has got a pair of gray britches and a black coat. mother said the rally was a good thing becaus it was the first time she had seen father dressed up since he was married.

Aug. 29. they was a big thunder shower last nite. we all got up in the nite and went into mothers room. mother set on the fether bed and all them that was scart cood set there. i wasent scart. father said it wood be jest the cussid luck to have it rane the nite of the rally.

Aug. 30. we had the last practise tonite, father put on his best close and new boots and the girls had on their plad dresses and i had on a new paper coller. we all set down and father came in and stood up. i tell you he looked fine. well he begun, mister modderater had i suposed or for 1 moment dremp, and then he forgot the rest. i tell you he was mad. i wanted to laff but dident dass to. well after a while he remembered and went through it all rite, and then he went over it 2 times more. gosh what if he shood forget it tomorrow nite. he is going to wright some of it on his cufs and he prac-

tised tonite making jestures so as to bring
his cufs up so that he cood read it.

Aug. 31. The rally is tonite. father woke
us all up last nite hollering in his sleep. he
dremp about the speach. this morning he
went to Boston without eating his brekfast.
i gess he is begining to be scart. i am a
going to make his boots shine today. gosh
what if he shood brake down. i gess i am
getting a little scart too. brite and fair.

Sept. 1. Last nite father came home and
the first thing he did was to send me down
to Miss Pratts for his shert. it was all pol-
lished and shone like glass. then he asked
if i had blacked his boots and then he et
supper. he dident eat much though. he said
Mr. Tuck came down from Boston with him.
Mr. Tuck was a going to make a speach first
and then he was going to introduce Gim

128

Loverin as chairman and then Gim Loverin
was a going to call on father. father said he
bet 5 dollars he wood call him Gim instead
of mister modderater. father was pretty cross
at supper. i gess he was getting scart. the
baby began to cry and father asked mother
why she dident choak the squawling brat
and mother sorter laffed and put the baby
into fathers lap and said i gess you had
better choak him. father laffed and began to
toss the baby up and down. he likes the
baby and while he was playing with it he
was all rite. but after supper he was cross
and said he hed a auful headake. then he
went practising his speach again so as not to
call the modderater Gim. well we got ready
and went down erly to get some good seats
so as to hear father and see him come in
with them that was to set on the platform.

129

we wanted to go down with father but he said he coodent bother with us. but before we went he came down stairs with his new close on and he looked fine but his face looked auful white. he said he had a headake but as soon as he got started to speak it wood all go off. so we went down. Cele had her hair curled and Keene had a new red silk ribbon on her hair becaus her hair wont curl and Aunt Sarah had on a new dolman with beeds on it and some long coral earrings and they all looked fine. Aunt Sarah took Georgie by the hand becaus she was the littlest and me and Keene and Cele followed on.

When we got there the band was playing in front of the town hall and aunt Sarah said i cood stay out and hear it and then said i cood sit with Gim Wingit and Willy

130

Swet if i wood behave. i said i wood and we
lissened and after the band went in we went
too. most all the seats were taken and we
got some bully seats way up front. i looked
for father but coodent see him becaus the
speakers hadent come in. well jest as soon
as we got in the policeman was up in front
and he said they has been too much whisling
and stamping and the next one that whisles
or stamps will get put out. well they was
old Swane and Brown and Kize and Dirgin
and every body kept quiet. after a few
minits the band began to play hale to the
chief and the speakers came marching up the
middle ile. i looked for father but he wasnt
there. evrybody began to clap and stamp
and Gim and Willy asked me where my old
man was. i stood up to see if he was there
and jest then i saw the policeman a rushing

at me. he grabed me by the collar and shook
me round till i dident know which end my
head was on and he draged me down the ile
and threw me out. as we were going down
the ile i saw Aunt Sarah running down the
other ile as fast as she cood go with her bon-
net on the back of her head and Keene and
Cele and Georgie following along all bawling. she got out in the entry jest as he was
going to put me out of the front door and
she grabed me away from him and said you
misable cowardly retch to treat a boy that
way. he said i whisled and she said he
dident and you knew it only you dident
dass take ennyone else.

Then she told us to come home and we
went home as fast as we cood all bawling.
when we got home mother was sitting
up alone and aunt Sarah started to tell

her and Keene and Cele and Georgie all
bawled and you never heard such a noise,
and father was in bed with a headake and
hollered out what in time is the matter. and
she told him and i heard him jump out of
bed and in a minit he came out buttoning
up his suspenders. Mother said where in
the world are you going George, and he said
things is come to a pretty pass if a boy cant
go and hear his father make a speach without being banged round by a policeman.
i am going down to knock the heads off
every policeman there. and he reeched for
his vest. mother said George, dont you go
near the hall, and father said he cood lick
anny 2 men on the police force easy and he
would show them how to slam people round
and he reeched for his coat, and Keene and
Cele and Georgie began to bawl again to

think he wood get hurt and aunt Sarah and
mother said you had better not go George,
and father said he wood give them more fun
in 5 minits than they had seen in a political
rally in 5 years and he reeched for his boots
and mother said what will they think of you
after you have sent word that you are too
sick to make a speach, to see you come rushing into the hall and go punching the policemen and father had got on 1 boot and when
she said that he began to look kinder sick
and said, thunder that is so. and then his
headake got wirse and he gave me a twenty
five cent scrip and Keene and Cele and
Georgie ten cents each and he went to bed
and so did we.

i wonder if his head aked realy so he
coodent make a speach or if he was scart.
i bet he was scart.

134

school commences monday. father hasent asked once about my diry, so i aint going to wright enny more.

Printed in the United States
32665LVS00001B/364-408